WE'LL MAIL OURSELVES TO YOU!

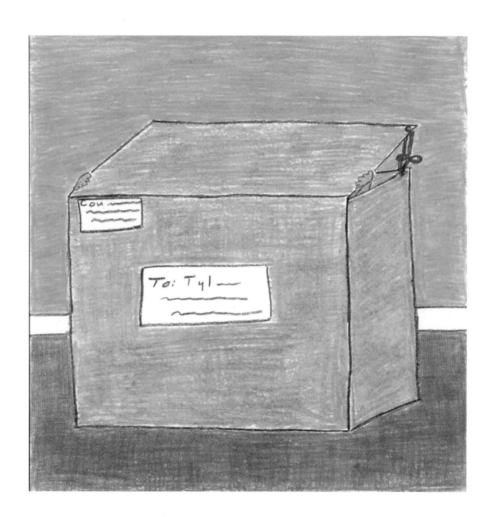

Written and Illustrated
By
Barbara Sonner

WE'LL MAIL OURSELVES TO YOU!

Publisher Copyright © 2011
Mimi Publishing, LLC
ISBN -13: 978-1466298965
ISBN-10: 1466298960

Dedicated to:
Hallie, Hanna,
Sonner, Leslie, Tyler,
Garrison, Calista

Dear Cousin Tyler,

   We really want to come visit you at your house. But Mommy and Daddy can't bring us right now. We've been thinking a lot about how we could get there. We heard a song that was about mailing someone to somebody. We are going to try it. If it works, we'll be there soon!

Love,
   Your Cousins

Dear Cousin Tyler,

   We are working on a plan to visit you soon.   We'll let you know how things are going.

   Love,

   Your Cousins

Dear Cousin Tyler,

    Our visit doesn't look too promising. We laid our big roll of art paper on the floor and pulled off a h-u-g-e, l-o-o-o-n-g piece. Gracie and I tried to roll the paper around us to make us into a package. What a mess! The paper kept tearing and wouldn't stay on. After that, it just got harder. Sonner and Leslie decided they wanted to be rolled up too. You can just imagine how silly things got. We tried rolling the paper around all of us. This time we used glue and tape on the paper to make it stick to us.

That sure made a mess! Everybody giggled, squiggled and kicked which ripped holes in the paper. It was so funny that even though I kept telling them, "Stop being silly so we can do this," I had to laugh too. They wouldn't even listen. Some of the paper stuck in our hair and on our clothes. But most of it was glued to the floor. There wasn't a piece of paper left big enough to put your address on to mail us. Oh well, we'll try again tomorrow. Love,

Your Cousins

Dear Cousin Tyler,

Today Gracie had a great idea. She found a box and said we could mail ourselves in it. We climbed inside. It got very dark when we closed the lid. So we tied it open a tiny bit. Finally . . . we decided we were ready to go. Then we thought of another problem. We didn't know how we could move the box outside to the mailbox.

Gracie came through with another idea. She said we could punch holes in the bottom of the box and stick our feet out. Then we could walk to the mailbox at the edge of our yard. That's when we discovered more problems. We couldn't get the box through the door, we couldn't walk down the porch steps, and we didn't know how many stamps to stick on the box.

Our biggest problem was a loud voice saying, "Somebody made a big mess and somebody needs to clean it up. " We climbed out of the box and cleaned the rest of the afternoon.

Love,

Your Cousins

Dear Cousin Tyler,
    We have travel problems. I don't think we can mail ourselves to you. Want to visit us?

Love,

    Your Cousins

P.S.
Don't let glue dry on the floor. It's hard to clean up. Wet mops can be really messy.

P.P.S.

We found out that the mail can only carry packages. People have to go in cars, trains, planes, or ships. That messed up our plan.

P.P.P.S.
To keep your mom happy, talk to her before you plan a trip. Moms can sure get overly excited about some plans.

THE END

About the Author

Barbara has seven grandchildren who enjoy spending time together playing, creating projects, and listening to stories. She likes to write stories to share with them when they visit with her in South Carolina.

79653681R00018